Grey
Island
Red Boat

Grey
Island
Red Boat

Ian Beck

Barrington Stoke

First published in 2016 in Great Britain by
Barrington Stoke Ltd
18 Walker Street, Edinburgh, EH3 7LP

www.barringtonstoke.co.uk

Text © 2016 Ian Beck
Illustrations © 2016 Ian Beck

A CIP catalogue record for this book is available
from the British Library upon request

ISBN: 978-1-78112-521-2

Printed in China by Leo

This book has dyslexia friendly features

For my grandson, Sebastian Beck

Contents

The Island of Ashes

A long time ago there was a grey island set in a grey sea. On the island there lived a princess. Her name was Opal and her home was a cold grey castle in the middle of a cold grey moat.

The castle towers were defended by six big grey cannons and a troop of grey soldiers. There were grey gardens, grey trees and grey flowers.

The name of the island was the Island of Ashes.

Princess Opal sat on her grey granite throne in a grey granite room at the top of one of the towers. She looked out to the far-off horizon and wished somehow for her life to be different.

Something was missing.

The cold grey sea washed up against the granite rocks at the shore just as it did every day.

Life was always the same for Princess Opal.

It was always November.

It was always grey, cold and wet.

Every day, her father, the King, went up into the sky in his grey hot air balloon and shouted at the rain to stop.

Every day, the island's fishermen landed their silver-grey fish in the harbour near the castle. Princess Opal would sneak down to the harbour in a long grey cloak just to have something lively to watch.

Then, one very wet grey afternoon, life turned out not to be always the same for Princess Opal.

A Strange Little Boat

That afternoon, a fisherman towed in a little boat that he had found adrift on the open sea. The little boat was not the usual kind of fishing boat. Its sails were ragged and torn. It was so small that there was only just room for one sailor.

Something else about the little
boat puzzled the princess. Its hull was
painted. It wasn't grey. It was a colour.

The hull of the little boat was
painted red.

This was something Princess Opal had never seen before.

The sight of the little red boat gave her eyes a kind of ticklish feeling. The ticklish feeling pleased the princess and made her smile. She liked it, but she couldn't say why. She ran on down to the harbour just in time to see the fisherman lift a young man out of the boat and lay him down by the shore.

The young man was about her
own age. He was bundled up in a grey
blanket that the fisherman had given
him for warmth. The fisherman turned
to look at Princess Opal.

"Excuse me, Princess Opal," he said
with a bow, "but does your father know
you are down here among us and the
fish?"

"Ssh," the princess said. "No, he doesn't. He's up there in his grey balloon, trying to stop the rain. Who is this?"

"I found him drifting in his boat far out at sea," the fisherman said. "No idea where he's from. He's not from here to be sure."

"His little boat looks so strange," Princess Opal said.

"That was why I first noticed it, Princess Opal. It is a very different sort of boat. I will say it fair tickled my eyes just to look at it."

"And mine," she said. "But the tickling was very nice. It made me feel warm inside and made me smile."

The young man stirred, sat up, and opened his eyes.

"He is awake," the princess said, "and he needs our care. Please help me to take him up to the castle."

"Are you sure?" the fisherman said.

"Yes, I am!" Princess Opal cried. "Come on."

And so Princess Opal and the fisherman helped the young man to his feet.

At first the young man seemed a bit unsteady. He stumbled on the steep path that led up to the grey castle gates. He held onto the branch of a grey tree to steady himself.

The princess reached out her hand to help him. He shook his head and spoke to her for the first time.

"No," he said. "Please, you mustn't touch me." He found his feet again and they walked on up to the gates.

As the fisherman walked back
down to the harbour, he noticed that
the dull grey leaves on the tree the
young man had touched had all turned
a bright green colour. First the little
red boat and now the green leaves. The
fisherman couldn't believe his eyes.

He ran to fetch some of the other fishermen to come and see the bright green tree for themselves.

Tickles and Smiles

The princess opened the castle gates.
The garden was empty and rain dripped
endlessly from the roof.

"Come on inside," the princess said,
"before you catch cold."

She took the young man to the empty throne room.

"You'll need some dry clothes," she said. "I'll see what I can find."

"There's really no need," the young man said. "I'm dry enough."

He took the grey blanket from around his shoulders. And when Princess Opal saw what he was wearing, her eyes tickled all over again. And again she smiled. The young man's clothes were so unusual, so bright. They weren't grey. They were like jewels shining in the sun. She laughed.

"What is it?" he said.

"Your clothes look so strange, but truly they please my eyes and my heart too."

"I am glad," he said with a smile. "My name, by the way, is Wendell Lightfoot."

"I am Princess Opal," she told him. "Welcome to my kingdom – the Island of Ashes."

"I am pleased to meet you, Princess Opal," Wendell Lightfoot said with a bow. "And I am pleased to be here, for I was banished, set adrift in my little red boat from my own homeland."

"Why would someone do that to you?" she said.

Wendell Lightfoot walked over to the tall windows of the throne room.

He reached out and put his hand to the hem of the long grey curtain.

The curtain changed before Princess Opal's eyes. It turned from grey to something else, something bright, something like sunshine. She had seen real sunshine only once, and that was years ago. It tickled the princess's eyes so much that she laughed out loud.

"They said I was cursed, that I was bewitched," Wendell said, "because of this."

"It looks more like a blessing to me," Princess Opal said, amazed by what he had done. At that moment the door opened and the King swept in with a troop of grey guards.

"Still raining non-stop," the King said as he shook rainwater from his robes. "Will it never end? Some fishermen just showed me the oddest thing," he went on. "One of our trees has somehow changed itself and all its leaves have gone very strange. It hurt my eyes to look at them, but the fishermen seemed very excited by it. They showed me a very odd boat too. Said it was all because of some stranger they found at sea ..."

Then the King noticed Wendell. He was still standing beside the window with Princess Opal. The curtains had also gone very strange and were now doing something to the King's eyes. He felt as if his eyes were being tickled.

"What on earth is going on?" he demanded. "Who is this young man and what is he doing in my kingdom?"

"Father, this is Mr Wendell Lightfoot," Princess Opal said, and her eyes sparkled. "Just look what he can do."

"I've seen what he can do and I don't much like it," the King said, and he shielded his eyes from the sunshine-coloured curtain.

"Take him down to the dungeons," he ordered the guards. "I will think what to do with him."

"No, Father, please, not the dungeons," Princess Opal begged, but it was no use.

The King's mind was made up. The grey guards grabbed hold of Wendell Lightfoot and dragged him down into the deep dark dungeons below the castle.

The Colour of Magic

The dungeons were cold and grey and damp, but at least Wendell Lightfoot had food and water down there. The Dungeon Master was the most miserable man in the kingdom, but soon he came back to the castle kitchens with a tray the colour of magic. On the tray was a bright plate, a bright cup and a bright spoon.

"He's a magician that Wendell," the Dungeon Master said. He was proud to show everyone what had happened to his grey things. "Those old iron dungeon bars fair tickle your eyes now as well," he added. "You should see it down there – it's as bright and cheery as a summer's day."

Such a Difference

News soon spread around the Island of Ashes about the stranger and his power to make everyday objects – things like mugs and trees and curtains and even fishing boats – bright enough to tickle your eyes in the nicest possible way.

It was not long before the fishermen came with a petition to the King.

"We would like our fishing boats to tickle our eyes just like the stranger's little boat," they said.

The Royal Gardener came and saw the King too.

"Your Majesty," he said, "I would so like it if all the trees in the castle garden could be green and glow like the one the stranger touched."

The King huffed and puffed. "Why does everybody want to change everything all of a sudden?" he said.

But he got no answer, for the Dungeon Master came to see him too. "Beg your pardon, Your Majesty," he said, "but young Wendell has made such a difference to my life down in my dark domain. I feel quite happy down there now, what with all the colours he's made."

"Colours?" the King said with a puzzled frown.

"Yes, colours," Princess Opal said, for she had come to see the King too. "That's what he calls the eye-tickling that he does. He adds colour to things."

"Well, I don't trust him or his colours," the King replied, "so I'm keeping him down in the dungeons."

The Dungeon Master

And so it was that Wendell Lightfoot was kept locked away in the King's dungeon, even though the only person who wanted to keep him down there was the King.

But whenever the King was up and away in his grey hot air balloon, shouting at the rain to stop, Princess Opal sneaked down to visit Wendell Lightfoot in the dungeons.

The rain still fell, of course, but Wendell's cell and the iron bars were full of colour now and ever so cheerful.

Princess Opal had grown to love the gentle Wendell and his gift of colour, and she was sure that he loved her too.

"If the Dungeon Master would only
let you out of here, then we could run
away together," Princess Opal said. "We

could take your little red boat from the harbour and set sail for somewhere new."

"We could," Wendell said, "but what about the grey guards and the six iron cannons and your bad-tempered father, the King?"

"Don't worry about him," Princess Opal said. "He's always cross. The non-stop rain every day has filled him with everlasting gloom."

"And the Dungeon Master," Wendell said. "Wouldn't he get into trouble?"

"Not if we made it look like you'd escaped and it wasn't his fault," she said.

The Dungeon Master was so happy with all the bright colours around him that he agreed to their plan right away. He even found them some rope so they could tie him up – but not too tight – and so Wendell escaped with Princess Opal.

Running Away Together

Wendell Lightfoot and Princess Opal ran off across the castle gardens. As they ran, Wendell touched every tree and shrub and flower. And they all, every one of them, burst into dazzling colourful life. The Royal Gardener shouted out in delight and waved them on with a cheery "thank you".

But the guards glared down from
the tower and shouted at them to stop.
"We'll fire the cannons," they yelled.

Wendell and Princess Opal ran even faster down the steep grey hill to the harbour.

It was raining hard as usual, so hard that the rain bounced off the grey boats, the grey sea and the grey harbour wall.

The boats were all tied up together and Wendell's little red boat was at the furthest end of the jetty.

The fastest way to get to it was to jump down onto the first fishing boat and then run and jump from one boat to the next until they reached the little red one. As Wendell jumped from boat to boat, each boat changed.

They stopped being dull and grey, and they became as bright and shiny as jewels.

They were –

Yellow

Red

Blue

Green

Violet

Orange ...

On and on, all different colours.

The fishermen cheered and called out "thank you" as Wendell and Princess Opal jumped and ran across the boats.

But before they could reach the little red boat there was the sound of cannon fire from the castle. *Boom!* The little red boat was smashed and sunk. Wendell and Opal ran up the steep harbour steps.

The grey clouds were so low now that they almost touched the castle tower.

The King climbed out of his grey weather balloon and tied it up near the harbour wall.

The rain was falling harder than ever and he was very cross indeed. To make matters worse, his daughter was running towards him across the grey grass with that dangerous fool, Wendell Lightfoot.

"What on earth are you doing, Opal?" the King said.

"Running away, Father," she cried above the noise of the rain. "Wendell and I are running away together."

As if by way of reply, there was another burst of cannon fire and a great iron cannon ball splashed into the sea.

"I am sorry, Your Majesty, but it's true," Wendell said. "No cannon will stop us, for we love each other."

He reached out and touched the
King's grey robes. At once they turned
many colours with a shiny gold trim.
The crown on the King's head went from
iron grey to flashing gold and the grey
glass blobs around the edge of the crown
were turned into gleaming red rubies.

"Oh," was all the King could say. He looked down at his robes and lifted the crown from his head. "Well I never! Just look at that ... oh my goodness." He was lost for words, but he was smiling now, a real smile for the first time that Princess Opal could remember.

"There," she said, "now you look like a proper king."

Wendell and Opal hopped into the basket of the balloon and together they untied the rope that held it to the ground. The balloon lifted into the wet grey sky.

"Hey," the King called out. "I'm sorry! Come back! Please come back!"

The King, the guards and the fishermen all watched as the balloon, now the same bright red colour as Wendell's little boat, lifted up into the grey sky.

Sunshine and Rain

Boom! The cannon fired again.

"No," the King called out. "Stop! No more cannon fire."

The cannon ball just missed the red balloon. It tore a great hole in the low

grey cloud. Wendell reached up and touched the ragged wet edge of the cloud. He pushed at it and the hole in the sky got bigger.

There was blue behind the rainy grey clouds. And in the blue there was a big ball of golden light.

"Sunshine," Wendell said, "and rain, look."

He reached both arms up into the blue and a great arc of colours – red, orange, green, blue, indigo and violet – spilled out all over the sky.

The grey rain clouds parted.

The sun shone down on the Island of Ashes. The King stood in his purple robes and his gold crown and looked out over his kingdom.

The hills and fields were green. The trees were green. The flowers were a jumble of bright colours. The sea was a deep blue.

Above it all was the arc. An arc of so many colours in the bright blue sky. And then the arc of colours faded away and at last the rain stopped.

It was warm in the sunlight. All the colours tickled the King's eyes so much that he smiled and laughed and cried a little bit all at the same time.

"Come back, my dear Opal and young Wendell," he called out, as loud as he could. "I'm sorry."

And, sure enough, the red balloon drifted down from the clear blue sky.

The Royal Gardener ran up to the King with a big bunch of sweet-smelling yellow roses.

"Here, Your Majesty," he said. "These are for Princess Opal. She might like them for her adventures."

"Why, yes, I think she will," the King said.

The guards in the tower fired the cannon again. But this time it was a salute for Wendell Lightfoot and Princess Opal. The guards' uniforms were now ruby red and the cannon glinted like gold.

The sun shone down on Wendell Lightfoot and Princess Opal as they sailed away in a little red boat which bobbed and dipped on the bright blue sea.